MW01531211

GRILLED TO BITS

STREET FOOD COZIES, BOOK 7

GRETCHEN ALLEN

SUMMER PRESCOTT BOOKS PUBLISHING

CHAPTER ONE

The boat rocked lightly side to side. Billie Halifax set her glass down on the table and gripped the edge, hoping the nausea passed over her before her host and partner served the main course. Asher Scanlan appeared from below deck carrying a steaming casserole dish and set it down about six inches from her plate.

Billie inhaled the steamy aroma from the casserole and jumped to her feet. She raced to the end of the bow and doubled over the railing. She stood up slowly and rested her forehead on the cool metal before turning back to Asher.

"If you didn't want to eat dinner with me, all you had to do was say it," he said.

"Please don't mess with me," Billie said. She

made her way back to the table and sat down. "I don't feel well."

"I can tell," Asher said. He picked up the casserole and walked back downstairs to the kitchen. Billie maintained her composure while he was gone. At that moment, maintaining her composure meant simply staying upright in her chair.

"I have no idea what's wrong with me," she said when he returned from below.

"Have you had anything at all to eat today?" he asked her.

Billie nodded her head. "I interviewed a manager for the newest food truck," she said. "Alex Regent picked the candidate from the culinary school on the mainland, and I think he picked a doozy."

"What makes you think that?"

"For one thing, she spent the first twelve minutes of the interview extolling the virtues of veganism," Billie said. "Which, let's be honest, is not a good look for the manager of a gourmet burger food truck."

"Did you eat something she made?" Asher asked. His eyebrows knit together in concern.

Billie nodded her head. "Yeah. She made three sliders for me, and I sampled each of them," she said, placing her hand on her stomach. "That was about two hours ago."

"Have you had anything else besides that?"

"No, nothing," Billie said. "The funny thing is, I can't get in touch with her now."

"The food truck manager?" Asher asked her.

Billie nodded again. "She was supposed to come back and share the rest of her menu with me, but she never showed up. That's why I was able to meet you for dinner."

"Wow. So, she never showed or called?"

"Nope. I haven't heard a single word from her. I'm starting to think she skipped town."

"What about Alex? Have you spoken to him about any of this?"

"I sent him a text, but no, I haven't much felt like talking to anyone," she admitted. "I know I have to call him at some point, though. I don't think this girl is going to work out."

"What's her name?"

"Julie Neilson."

"Was she staying on the island?" Asher asked.

Billie herself had been a resident of Sea Glass Island off the Florida coast for about a year and half. In that time, she had become as much of a local as if she had been born and raised there.

"The mainland. I called the hotel she mentioned she was staying at," she said weakly. "They couldn't tell me if she was still there, but they also wouldn't put me through to her room."

"You need to call Alex," Asher said. "But not until after we get you to urgent care. I think you might have food poisoning."

Billie let Asher lead her off the boat and back onto the dock. Luckily, they had remained at the marina for their dinner date. Billie wobbled on her feet when they made it to the wooden walkway. "Oh," she said and hesitated. She leaned forward and placed her hands on her knees. "I don't know if I can make it to the parking lot. We have to go slow."

"Stay here," Asher said. He left her with her hands on the thick dock rope and disappeared back to the boat. Billie had little choice but to do as he asked. She held on tight to the scratchy rope, thicker than the span of her hand.

"Try to drink this," Asher commanded when he returned. He pressed a bottle to her lips. Billie sipped the ice-cold liquid and closed her eyes.

"What is that?" she asked when she regained herself.

"Electrolytes," Asher said. "Like the stuff they give little kids when they're sick."

"You just happened to have that on board?" Billie asked with a small chuckle. She was still holding onto the rope and grabbed on tighter when she realized that any form of laughter was too much for her to take.

"Best remedy for a hangover," Asher said with a smile. "I've always kept this on hand wherever I've lived, ever since college."

"That tells me a whole lot about you." Billie stood upright. "I think I can make it if we seriously go really slowly." Asher carried the bottle in one hand and hooked the other arm around her back. He gently led her down the dock and into the parking lot.

They arrived at the urgent care clinic a short time later. Fortunately, there was no one else in the waiting room, so Billie was able to go straight in to visit the nurse. She returned with a prescription and instructions to go home and rest for at least twelve hours.

"They think I may have some sort of bacterial poisoning," she told Asher. "I have to take antibiotics in case there was something wrong with the meat. They also took several vials of my blood to have it tested."

"Better safe than sorry," Asher said. He drove her to the pharmacy and then back to the festival grounds where her tiny home was parked. Billie held on as he drove past the large, metal building that housed the commissary kitchen where her food truck managers prepped and tested their food truck menus.

"What's going on out here?" Polly Sheridan stepped out of the fifth wheel she'd been renting from Asher. Polly was one half of the team that ran the gourmet ice cream food truck. When she'd first started, she and her twin sister, Liza, were less than tolerant of one another. At the suggestion of Billie, the sisters had begun to live apart, thus making everyone's working experience that much better.

Waffles, Billie's spoiled Tibetan Mastiff, barked at the three of them as they chatted.

"I think I have food poisoning," Billie muttered as she unlocked her front door and stumbled inside. She could hear Asher and Polly still talking, but she ignored them and dragged herself to her small bathroom, pulling the door partially shut behind her.

Billie had lost track of time, but at some point, Asher and Polly worked together to guide her to her bed. She groaned while Polly removed her shoes. Asher helped her out of her thick sweatshirt and into her pajamas. Polly disappeared to the kitchen and returned with a large bowl for her bedside, just in case.

She woke four more times before the end of the night, alternating between freezing beneath the covers and burning up. Two days later, her headache had subsided, and she found enough strength to make it to her feet. She checked her phone for any messages but found nothing of importance. She sent a quick text to Julie, hoping for a reply, and pushed the barn door to the side that divided her bedroom area from the rest of the house.

Asher was fast asleep on her couch. Billie tiptoed past him and slipped into the bathroom. She splashed cold water on her face and brushed her teeth. She cracked the bathroom door again and checked on Asher, who was still sleeping. Billie shut the door again and slipped out of her clothes for a fast shower.

"Feeling better?" Asher asked when she came back out of the bathroom. He was standing in her kitchen. "Do you want some coffee?"

"I don't know if I'm ready for that just yet," Billie said with a chuckle. "I think I might want to gather everyone together in the big kitchen this morning, though. At least, I'd like to try to make that happen."

"Are you sure you're feeling up to it?" Asher asked.

"No, but I'm not feeling too bad right now, so I'm gonna give it a shot."

"Why do you want everyone together?"

"Well, for one, I want to talk about Julie and see if anyone else has had any luck getting in touch with her," Billie said. "And secondly, I want to crowd-source ideas for a replacement manager."

"Have you reached out to Alex again?" Asher asked her.

Billie shook her head. "I sent him that one message before I got really sick, but that's it. I have to be honest, about something though. He might be the executor of my grandmother's will and the liaison to the culinary school, but I have my doubts about his ability to pick a food truck manager. We've had problems with almost all of them in one way or another."

"But everything has worked out in the end," Asher pointed out.

"Maybe so, but this time feels different. And not in a good way."

CHAPTER TWO

Billie knocked lightly on the door of the RV next door.

A moment later, Polly answered. "You look pale. I mean, good morning."

Billie laughed. "I know I look terrible, but I'm feeling better. Anyway, I just came by to let you know that I'm going to send out a text to everyone to ask them to meet me at the commissary kitchen in a little while."

Polly raised a brow. "Is everything okay?"

"I'm not sure, but I did want to ask you if you've seen or heard anything from Julie Neilson, the new manager I met with a couple of days ago."

"No," Polly said. "I saw her briefly when she was

in the kitchen with you that first day, but I haven't run into her anywhere else or heard from her."

"Okay," Billie said. "I'm worried about her, but I'm also worried about the burger truck. I tried reaching out to her before I got sick, but I never heard a thing back."

Polly leaned against the doorway. "I'm sorry, but I have to ask. Do you think she deliberately made you sick?"

Billie shook her head. "I'm not prepared to make that claim just yet, but I am going to talk with Detective Sullivan this morning. I need to let her know that we can't reach Julie and something bad might have happened."

"Is that just your overactive imagination talking, or do you have reason to think something bad happened?" Polly asked.

Billie shrugged. "I have no idea, but I do want to keep Sully in the loop just in case. I'll see you later at the kitchen, okay?"

She left Polly's front door and headed across the festival grounds to the commissary kitchen. She was eager to get back to work after being out. Since her arrival on the island, Billie had seen gatherings of all sorts on the grounds. A few festivals, annual religious or cultural in nature, were on the calendar for the second time since she moved to Sea Glass Island from Boston, Massachusetts. She had lost track of the varieties of festivals she had seen. A new one was on the calendar nearly every week.

The coming festival focused primarily on the historical nature of cattle ranches in the state of Florida. The cattlemen's organization and other groups planned three days of demonstrations and speakers, and everyone in attendance would expect a great deal of food. It was the perfect setting for the debut of her burger truck, and now she had no manager to run it.

Billie had an idea of what to expect from the gathering, even though it was the first time the group had booked space on the island for their annual event. Back in her culinary school days, she had attended a similar event north of Tampa, although it was on a much smaller scale, she assumed. She was happy she had an idea of what to expect and what the participants would expect of her.

She stopped just before going inside to text her staff, and call Detective Sullivan.

"Good morning, Billie," Sully said. Her voice was husky and sleepy.

"Morning," Billie said, somewhat apologetically. "I wanted to give you a heads-up. My newest food truck manager is MIA this morning. Well, really since a couple of days ago. I'm going to send a photo over to you as soon as we get off of the phone."

"Okay, what can you tell me about this?" Sully asked, suddenly sounding much more alert.

"Her name is Julie Neilson. She's young and she was supposed to take on the new burger truck," Billie said. "We were together at the commissary kitchen so she could demonstrate her menu plans for me. She ended up making just three simple sliders using our ingredients and was supposed to be back that afternoon to go over the full menu, but she never showed up."

"So, are you saying she's missing or that the demonstration didn't go well, and she decided not to take on the job?"

"That's the thing. I don't technically know if she's missing. Normally, I wouldn't be too concerned but not only is she supposed to debut the truck soon, but I also have reason to believe that those sliders of hers gave me food poisoning."

"Are you suggesting it was on purpose?" Sully asked slowly.

"Almost as soon as I ate what she prepared, I started feeling sick. A few hours later, I was at urgent care being treated for food poisoning. That's all I know for sure."

"I see. Did the two of you have any issues while you were together?"

"Not that I know of. I was rather leery of her being a vegan, but we didn't argue about it or anything, if that's what you mean."

"Hmm, a vegan running a burger truck is rather interesting…"

"No kidding," Billie said. "Either way, I think me getting sick could be an important detail to know if she is missing."

"Alright. Thanks for letting me know," Sully said. "Can you give me what contact info you have for her? And how about a quick description?"

Billie did so and sighed, thankful the detective was there to help. She hung up the phone and headed inside, bypassing her office, and going straight for the kitchen areas. She wanted to check the cooler to see if she could figure out what ingredients Julie had used. As far as she was concerned, every single item in the commissary kitchen was safe, but she had to be sure.

She checked the common cooler, then went toward the larger coolers and freezers in the building. A quick walk around and a scan of the shelves revealed nothing aside from the typical ingredients left by the other truck managers. Each had his or her own individual space, and the overstock ingredients all appeared to be fine. Polly and her twin sister, Liza, stored gallons of heavy cream next to Enid Greene's farm fresh eggs and varieties of chocolate for the bakery mousse truck. Isa Carello stacked her premade marinara sauce next to containers of fresh mozzarella cheese.

Only her sushi truck manager and the barbecue truck team had large quantities of meat stacked up in their spaces. She knew right away what belonged to whom and nothing looked out of place. Carl Kensington's sushi preps came straight from the fish market down by the marina, and his exotic varieties of fish from the transport truck were on the shelves as well. Dillon Frazier and his sous chef, Olivia Mason, stored pounds of marinating meat destined for the smoker. Billie carefully moved aside the large tubs of marinating brisket and ribs just to make sure there was nothing stacked behind them. All she found was more brisket and ribs. She sighed and turned back to the door and headed for the kitchen.

"Is everything okay?" Enid asked when she met her on the other side of the cooler door. "Are you still sick?"

"I'm feeling better, and I was just checking to see if our new manager left anything in the cooler," Billie said. Normally, the managers supplied their own food on the first day, or used just a few ingredients from the kitchen, but Julie hadn't come with anything.

"Is that what you wanted us here to talk about this morning?" Enid asked.

"Yes, that and more," Billie said. She followed Enid to the larger space in front of the test kitchens where the tables and chairs were situated.

"Good morning, Marcel," Billie said to her taco truck manager. He had been with her the longest and she was grateful for the steady work ethic he brought to her fleet of food trucks. Not that she had favorites, but Marcel and Dillon were good candidates for that role if she did.

"Good morning," Isa and Carl said in unison.

"Good morning, everyone," Billie called out. Asher appeared in the kitchen just then. He winked at Billie and began making coffee in one of the restaurant-sized pots. As soon as the coffee maker started brewing, he turned and headed back down the hallway. Billie silently hoped he was going after some sort of sustenance. Her growling stomach had surprised her. She hadn't eaten more than a cracker or two since she started feeling sick, but food hadn't exactly been at the top of her list.

"Why are we all here?" Olivia asked. She took a

seat across the table from Dillon. 'Are you feeling better?"

She started off by assuring her team that she was still feeling a little under the weather, but things were much better than before. She appreciated their concern but had more pressing matters to deal with.

"I'm not sure how many of you met Julie Neilson," Billie began. She waited while a few of them mumbled their answers. "Julie prepared a few sliders for me to demonstrate her skills, as each of you have done upon your arrival to the island. Well, the long and short of it is that I can't get in touch with her now."

"Did anything weird happen at her demonstration?" Carl asked.

Billie shrugged. "She spoke about how she's a vegan, which was strange for someone taking over a burger truck. She didn't bring any ingredients with her, and she seemed a little nervous, but I didn't really think too much of it at the time. I know interviews can be nerve wracking."

"You should tell them the rest of it," Asher said. He had returned with two large boxes of donuts. "I got a couple of plain donuts for you."

"Thanks," Billie said, wondering if she could

stomach them. "First things first. Everyone grab a donut and have some coffee."

Asher opened the boxes and began filling mugs with coffee. Billie picked a donut out of the box and got herself a cup of water before she headed back to her seat. She took a small bite, and that was more than enough for her.

"What's the rest of it?" Dillon asked as soon as he took his seat across from her.

"Billie may have been poisoned by Julie," Asher offered.

"What exactly did the doctor say when you went?" Olivia asked. Billie could see the wheels in her head begin to turn. As a former police officer, her training kicked in from time to time.

"They confirmed that it was food poisoning and put me on antibiotics. I didn't eat anything but those sliders."

"How do you know the meat or one of the other ingredients wasn't bad?" Enid asked her.

"I don't, but like I said, she used our ingredients. I like to think we keep a very close eye on our food around here. Also, we've had our fair share of trouble in the past, and I just can't be too careful. I'm not blaming her, but it's crossed my mind. Does that make sense?"

Everyone nodded and spoke at once.

"Has anyone heard anything from Julie?" Asher interrupted. "That's one of the main reasons we wanted to gather all of you here."

"I never met her," Dillon said. Carl and Marcel both chimed in and said the same.

"I saw her in passing," Enid said. "Isa and I were here while she was setting things up."

"Enid and I spent a good part of the day at the beach, though, so we weren't here for long," Isa said. Her normal Hollywood good looks had only improved by her time in the sun.

"Polly and I said a few words to her," Liza Sheridan said. Polly nodded to confirm.

"But no one spent much time speaking with her?" Billie asked.

The twins shook their heads. "Only a couple of hellos. That's all," Polly said.

"Okay," Billie said. She looked up in time to see the red-headed detective enter the kitchen area.

"Hello, Sully," Asher said.

"Hi, everyone," Sully said. "I overheard your discussion. Does anyone have any idea where Julie was staying?"

Not one of them nodded their heads.

"Just her cell number and the name of the hotel

she may or may not have been staying at," Billie said. "But I already gave you that."

Sully nodded. "What about social media? Anyone?"

Again, she was met with shaking heads. "I don't even think I knew her last name until now," Olivia said.

"Did something else happen?" Asher asked the detective.

Billie looked at her. She hadn't considered that something else might have happened in the short time since she'd spoken to the detective.

"I had a call from the mainland," Sully said. "Sheriff Ken Avery returned my call about missing persons. Avery was just elected and took over about a week ago. I guess this is as good of a time as any for him to get to know us here on the island."

"What did he say?" Billie asked. She felt a sinking feeling in her middle.

"Can we talk in your office?"

Billie nodded and directed her there. "What happened?"

Sully sighed and took a seat. "I'm only telling you this in case you think of something that can help. Ken told me that the body of a young woman was found early this morning at the bus station not far from where you thought Julie was staying. The woman wasn't carrying any identification with her at the time, so there's been no ID yet, but based on your description, it's possible it's the same person."

"Oh," Billie said. "Wow."

"So far, the cause of death has not been released," Sully said. "But it is suspicious, which is cop talk for homicide, if you didn't already know."

"I hate to have to ask this, but am I a suspect?"

Sully chuckled. "Not currently, but I would like to get an official statement from you and your crew. It's a bit early for all of that, and it might not matter, but I'd like to have it done just in case."

"I know the sheriff is just doing his job, but if it was Julie found out there, I can't imagine something happened to her on this island."

"That may be true, but like I said, I'd like to get the statements."

"You're right," Billie said. "I'm happy to give one and I'm sure everyone else will be too. Let's head back out there and you can do whatever you need to do."

They went back to the kitchen and faced a curious group, eagerly awaiting their return. Billie told them they'd each be giving a statement and Asher stood first, walking away with the detective.

"What are you going to do about the burger truck?" Dillon asked. "With the Cattle Rancher Festival coming up, I can't imagine that you're going to want to see the burger truck sitting idle."

"It has to debut. Have you seen that thing? Nolan did a terrific job on this one," Marcel said, making his opinion clear. Since his own taco truck debuted, it had become a tradition for the other truck managers to check out each new addition to the fleet.

"I have seen it," Billie teased. "I hope we can find a manager for the truck in time, but I'm not so sure. We're kind of cutting it close at this point."

With every truck, Billie was excited to see the big reveal when the truck was finished. The burger truck exterior was painted in a sharp combination of dark red and yellow. The name of the food truck, *Burger Bus*, was written in white on the side of the truck.

Billie was excited about the large serving window and colorful awning. Nolan, the food truck remodeler extraordinaire, had added a stainless steel shelf below the serving window where the manager, whoever that ended up being, would be able to set condiments and other ingredients on the self-serve shelf for convenience.

Inside the truck was fitted with a pair of large, gas-powered grills. Nolan had become an expert at creating large amounts of storage and preparation space inside the small areas.

"What are you going to do if Julie reappears?" Dillon asked. "Does she still have a job with us?"

Billie shook her head. "I don't think so," she said. "I don't have one hundred percent proof that she made me sick, but I don't think I'm willing to take a risk with our customers."

After the rest of the group went through their interviews, Sully came to talk to Billie.

"I took a page from your book and took a look at the missing woman's social media pages. It appears she was an outspoken critic of the meat industry. I don't know who recommended her for the job as your burger truck manager, but whoever it was, didn't vet her very well."

Billie nodded. "My grandmother's attorney, Alex Regent, is the one who sets all of that up for me," she said. "And he is not on social media, as far as I can tell."

"Billie, if you're needing someone to come and take over the truck for the time being, I have a buddy who lives on the mainland who might be able to help," Dillon offered. "He used to own a restaurant. Gourmet burgers are sort of his thing."

Her eyes widened. "He used to own a restaurant. What does he do now?" she asked. "Is he available?"

Dillon nodded. "He teaches seminars at the culinary school just like I was doing when Alex reached out to me," he said. "And he works in a library now as well."

"I don't mean to interfere here or anything. This is Billie's business, after all," Asher spoke up. "But why isn't he still in the restaurant business? I just want to make sure we don't have another situation if she picks this guy to come and take over."

"All legit questions," he said. "The most I can tell you is that he had a business partner who took the money and ran away with it, and he was pretty devastated."

"What's his name?" Billie asked. She couldn't help but smile. Anyone recommended by Dillon was bound to be a professional.

"Cameron Shields," Dillon said. "I'll give him a call and introduce the two of you right away."

\

CHAPTER THREE

Billie spent the remainder of the day helping out where she could. Despite the nature of the festival, each of the food trucks would move from their permanent positions on the boardwalk near the beach and relocate to the festival grounds.

She wondered if she should try again for an evening meal on the boat with Asher. She never wanted to smell that particular casserole ever again, but she was ready to get some real food in her stomach. Thankfully, her bout of food poisoning wasn't as bad as it could have been.

When the Sheridan twins finished their last preparations for the ice cream truck, Billie checked the cooler for her favorite homemade treat, wine-soaked pear ice cream, which the twins were known to leave for her here and there. She smiled when she found two small dishes, one for herself and one for Asher. Or one for later. There was no name on the dishes, and no rules. Billie decided that she could take both back to her house, and if both disappeared before Asher knew they existed, well, he should have checked the cooler first.

"You can wait one second, mister," Billie said to Waffles when she walked by his pen on her way home. Her arms were full, and he whimpered when she passed him up. Billie rushed inside and threw the ice cream in her freezer. She set her bag down and quickly changed into her favorite workout clothes.

Billie had finally figured out the right shoes to wear when she hit the beach for a walk, or a run depending on Waffles' temperament. For a long time, she'd walked in leather huaraches, but after a lot of trial and error, she had at last settled on a lightweight trail shoe that did the trick.

She grabbed the leash from the hook by the front door and headed back outside. She opened the gate and hooked the leash on the fluffy pooch's collar. Waffles jumped up and down in place while he waited for Billie to free him from his prison. She glanced at the extra-large dog mansion she'd had assembled for him. His existence was such a terrible one, after all.

They walked toward the gate separating the festival grounds from the beach. A light breeze blew over them off of the gulf. She smiled and picked up her pace. Waffles complied and trotted along in front of her, pausing only to bark at seagulls as he passed by them. They headed away from the marina and the condo side of the island. Billie found the south side of the island to be her favorite. She loved gazing out into the open water, especially when she could see large vessels passing in the shipping lane.

Billie waited until she reached the open dog beach and unhooked Waffles from his leash. He took off running for the water and jumped into the shallow waves as they splashed against the shore. They enjoyed a small space on the beach away from others. She could hear the laughter of onlooking children as the large dog barked and chased after crabs on the beach. Once in a while, the tables turned, and a crab would turn and run after him. Billie chuckled when he panicked and took off running from the tiny crustaceans.

After several minutes, she called the dog back to her and reattached the leash. They walked a little bit further down the beach before she turned and headed home. Her phone rang just as they were arriving. She checked her screen. Rhonda was calling her. Billie decided to wait until she had had Waffles settled before she did anything else.

"Get in there," she said to Waffles when he decided he wasn't finished playing. She unhooked the leash and led the dog inside. Waffles barked and ran around in a circle, trying to tempt her into playing. Billie patted him on his head and pointed to the living room where he promptly huffed and flopped down on the floor in front of her small couch.

After she hung the leash back up on the hook, Billie kicked off her shoes and sat down on the couch to return Rhonda's call. She was surprised to see that she had not left a voicemail. Even so, she dialed her number and waited for her to pick it up.

"Billie?" Rhonda answered on the second ring.

"Yeah, sorry I didn't answer before," Billie said. "Waffles and I just got back from our walk."

"I have some news," Rhonda said.

"Oh, no. What about?"

"Asher told me about what's been going on, and well, I have a friend who works down at the bus station."

"What do you know?" Billie asked.

"He's a bit of a gossip hound, and not everything he says is reliable, but he overheard some officers talking and he thinks it was your manager who was killed."

"How would he know that?"

"Not only did he say she had some papers from the festival grounds on her, but he heard the name Julie mentioned quite a few times and that's the name Asher told me. Like I said, it might not be right, but I thought you might want to know."

Billie didn't like rumors much, but any sort of news could help so long as she kept in mind that it wasn't official news.

"Did your friend happen to say what happened to the victim?"

"He said she had marks all over her neck like she was strangled," Rhonda said.

Billie frowned. "Don't bus stations have cameras? No matter who the body belongs to, there must be a suspect already."

"I have no idea about any of that," Rhonda admitted. "Maybe, whoever killed her did it at another location and then moved her there. This isn't really my department. I just wanted you to know."

"Where was she found?" Billie asked.

"That I do know. My friend said she was found on the outside of the terminal."

"So, they probably caught that on video," Billie said. "At least, I would think so. This sounds like a quick and easy case to solve."

"From what it sounds like, there are still missing pieces of this puzzle, I just hope that my information is a piece that can help."

Billie thanked Rhonda and ended the call after a few more minutes. All she knew was that she didn't kill anyone. Everything else was still up in the air.

As terrible as it was that it seemed the young woman from the culinary school had been found dead, Billie wondered if she would somehow wind up as the center of the police investigation after all. She was sure she had nothing to worry about, but there was always the chance that she was wrong. Another thought entered her mind. With everything going on, she had yet to speak with Alex to inform him about the status of the young woman he sent. As much as she hated to bring him the bad news, she wanted to get it done. He had to know what had occurred, from the food poisoning to Julie's possible death.

Billie scrolled through her contacts until she found Alex's number. She tapped the phone icon and waited while the phone rang. After five rings, his voicemail began.

"Alex, Billie Halifax here," she said. "I need to talk to you about the young woman you sent out here to run the burger truck for me. Call me back as soon as you can. Thanks." She hung up the phone and waited for a reply.

CHAPTER FOUR

"Billie, can you come to the kitchen really fast?" Asher texted her next. She got the feeling it wasn't about a cozy dinner on the boat.

She answered that she was on her way and got up from the couch. Waffles jostled when she stepped over him, thinking she was ready to play.

"You already had a walk, pup," Billie muttered. Just like she had already been to the commissary kitchen for the last time that evening, or so she'd thought. She carried her phone in her hand as she walked back toward the large, metal building.

Billie walked down the hall, past her office door. She could hear voices in the middle of the large kitchen space. It sounded like Asher speaking with another man. When she entered the space, she smiled at Asher and dropped her jaw at the sight of the other person.

Alex's wavy white hair stuck out in all directions. His white eyebrows turned upward like two fuzzy smiles and his mustache turned downward like a frown giving him a humorous, yet stern look.

He stepped toward her with his hand extended. "Billie, it's great to see you again."

She took Alex's hand and smiled. "Uhm, yes. Good to see you as well."

"I should have been here before now," Alex said seriously. "I hear you have found a friend in one of your grandmother's old pals."

Billie released his hand and nodded her head. "Rhonda has become a really good friend to me," she said.

"Your grandmother would be so happy to know that," Alex said.

Her mind was reeling. Why was Alex on the island? In all the time she'd lived there, he had not once made the trip to the commissary kitchen. Billie routinely sent updates and photos of the food trucks once they were remodeled. Once in a while, she sent sales reports and other reports of her progress, but by the way he was acting, it was clear that he had no idea what was going on.

She felt a little unsettled at his arrival. He stood in front of her smiling but saying nothing. Billie looked at Asher again, wondering what she was supposed to do next.

"Would you like a fresh cup of coffee, Alex?" Asher asked at last. Billie could have kissed him at that moment for breaking the ice. She quickly found herself wondering for the first time if her relationship with Asher would be an issue.

"I would love a cup of coffee," Alex said. He looked at Billie. "I need to speak with you for a moment, my dear."

"Okay," Billie said with a nervous smile. "Let's go over here." She led him to a table and pulled a chair out for him to take a seat.

"Please, ladies first," Alex said. He placed his hand on the back of the chair.

"What's going on?" Asher asked. Billie shot a grateful smile in his direction.

Alex took the coffee from Asher and blew on it before taking a sip. "I had a phone call with Phillip Abernathy just a bit ago and he was asking me questions about the woman who I sent out here to manage your newest truck."

"Okay," she said. "I actually tried calling you a bit ago to let you know that she's not only disappeared, but she might be dead. I also think she may have purposely made me sick with her food."

"Wait a minute," Alex said. He raised a single finger and pointed it at Billie. "Say that again and go much slower?"

Billie sighed. She had not looked forward to telling him about any of this and had hoped to do so over the phone. "When I get a new food truck manager, I generally ask for them to prepare a sampling of their menus for Asher and me to try out."

Alex nodded his head. "I am aware of this," he said.

"Well, Julie did not come prepared to do that," Billie continued. "Instead, she made three little sliders and used our ingredients. She promised to come back to go over the full menu, but she never showed up. Anyway, less than two hours after I ate the sliders I was sick. Very sick. I also just got a phone call from Rhonda, who said that she has reason to believe that the woman who was found dead at the bus station, is Julie."

"I had to take her to the urgent care," Asher said. "Wait, what?"

Billie explained her conversation with Rhonda and waited for someone to reply. Her own mind was reeling.

Alex nodded his head slowly. He narrowed his and glared into his coffee cup. "First, Billie, I am very sorry that happened to you," he said. "I take it you're better now?"

"Thanks to some fast-acting antibiotics, yes," she said.

"I'm glad to hear it. But there's something important you need to know. I don't know who it was that fixed you those sliders, or who is dead, but Julie Neilson never actually came out here. As a matter of fact, I left her back on the mainland with the head of the cooking school."

Billie stared at Alex. She could feel her jaw open but didn't have the energy or the wherewithal to close her mouth.

"Wait a minute," Asher said, breaking through the tension. "She never came here?"

Alex shook his head. "Correct," he said. "I didn't know until today that she changed her mind about the job."

"Why did she change her mind?" Billie managed to ask.

"She said she decided at the last minute that she didn't want to leave her mother and her sisters behind."

Billie could feel the chills rising up on her skin.

"Who cooked for me then, and who was at the bus station? It had to be the same woman who came here because Rhonda said she had papers from the festival grounds on her."

"We don't know that. It could have been anyone," Asher said.

"True, but this is all way too big of a coincidence. I mean, was someone from the culinary school so mad that Julie got the job over her that she found a way to convince Julie not to come and then come in her place?" Billie asked.

"If that was the case then she shouldn't have poisoned you," Asher pointed out.

Billie scoffed. "Yeah, but it explains why she'd come so unprepared."

Alex stood up and leaned across the table. "I have no idea who it was," he said. "I had assumed that Julie let you know she wasn't coming. She informed the instructors at the culinary school that she changed her mind, but I didn't know until today, like I said. I suppose someone could have convinced her not to come, as you said."

"Didn't Billie tell you that she met with the woman?" Asher asked. Billie nodded her head. She had sent a message to Alex.

Alex shook his head. "I don't think I saw a

message." He tapped around on his phone for a moment and frowned. "It's there. I'm sorry. I've just been so busy."

Billie tried to control her frustration. Someone in his position should pay more attention. "It's fine," she grumbled. "But what do we do now?"

"We have to let Detective Sullivan and the chief know about it," Asher said.

"The chief knows that the woman I planned to send never came," Alex said. He raised his hands and tried to calm the two of them down. "I'm sure he informed his staff the second I told him that she never left Florida."

"None of this makes a bit of sense," Billie said, shaking her head. "I just don't understand any of it."

CHAPTER FIVE

Dillon Frazier stood outside the front door of Billie's tiny house and knocked early the next morning. "I know it's way too early to be here," he said apologetically when she opened the front door. "But I thought you might like to know Cameron just showed up on the island, and he came prepared to create a feast for you."

"Right now?" Billie asked sleepily. "I'm not sure I can eat a burger before eight in the morning." She honestly wasn't sure she ever wanted to eat another burger again in her life, but she didn't think she could get away with that, especially now that she was feeling so much better.

"No, no," Dillon said. "Not right now. I just

wanted to let you know that he's in the kitchen preparing his menu."

"That's great," Billie said. "Why didn't you just text me about it, though?"

Dillon shook his head. "I guess you didn't hear," he said. "Phone towers are down all over the island. I don't think you can even get the internet to come up."

Billie opened her eyes a little wider. "The cell phone towers are down? Do you know why?" she asked.

"No clue," Dillon said. "There was a guy hanging around the kitchen waiting to speak with Asher. At first, I thought it was about the towers, but then he said his name was Frank something. He's part of that big group putting on the rancher's festival this weekend."

"Okay," Billie said, smiling. "I'll text Asher and let him know."

"I don't think you're going to text him," Dillon said with a smirk.

"Oh, yeah. It's definitely too early in the morning. My brain isn't working quite yet." She laughed. "I guess I'll have to run over there and tell him myself." She thanked Dillon and closed the door. Five minutes later, she was in her running shoes and had a leash in her hand. Waffles looked up at her and whined when she approached him. He sighed loudly and turned away from her.

"Hush. You can get up early once in a while. We're going to run across the beach to the marina and wake Asher up." At the mention of Asher's name, the dog jumped to his feet and began wagging his tail in excitement.

"Traitor," Billie said to him as she hooked the leash on his collar. She led him outside and headed for the gate. Once he figured out where they were going, he yanked her along behind him through the sand.

"Slow down!" When they got to the marina, Billie had to pull backward on the leash a bit. She breathed a little hard when they made their way to the boat slips. She was worn out, but after the revelation she received the night before, the exercise felt amazing. Billie slowed down when she approached the boat slips. She caught her breath as she made her way to Asher's boat. She climbed aboard and knocked on the door down to the cabin below deck. "Asher," she called out. "Hey, it's Billie." Waffles added a deep bark to announce his own presence.

"Billie?" Asher opened the door and climbed up on the bow. "I tried to call you."

"Cell phone towers are down all over the island,"

she said. "Dillon knocked on my door a half hour ago to let me know the new burger guy is already here. He also said some guy named Frank is waiting to talk to you. He's part of the rancher's organization, I guess."

"Oh, shoot," Asher said. "Be right back." He disappeared back down the steps. Waffles barked after him.

"Just wait," Billie said. "He's getting dressed."

Asher reappeared a few minutes later. "Sorry about that," he said. "I have to get over there and speak to Frank. He's not just part of the organization, he's the one in charge."

"Okay. And it's good news about Cameron, right? He's going to present his menu this afternoon in the kitchen. Maybe you can help me eat some of those burgers."

"Absolutely," Asher said. "It's great timing, too. Now I can reassure Frank that all of the food trucks will be ready to go when we open the festival."

"Is that why he wants to talk to you? Is he worried about something?"

"I don't exactly know why he wants to talk to me, but I do know that he's one of the most powerful members of the beef industry in the state of Florida."

"He sounds important," Billie said. "Haven't you worked with him before?"

Asher shook his head. "No, this is the first time, but I hope it's going to be the first of many," he said. "If we play our cards right, we might be able to keep these guys booked for future events. This is a really big deal."

They walked together toward the beach. Without a word, Asher took over the leash and slowed the dog's gait.

"I'll meet you at the kitchen," Billie said, taking the leash back from Asher when they arrived. "I need to feed Waffles and change my clothes before I run over to meet with Cameron or anyone else."

"Will you give him the job if he delivers?" Asher asked her.

Billie nodded. "As long as nothing too scary emerges from his past, I will beg him to join the team. We really need someone."

CHAPTER SIX

Dillon Frazier was seated on the tailgate of a navy blue pickup truck when Billie spotted him outside the commissary kitchen. She could smell the familiar aroma of the wood-burning smoker he used for his barbecue truck. Billie smiled and headed straight for him. Another man, tall but thinner and with thick, black hair turned to greet her when she approached.

"Billie Halifax, meet Cameron Shields," Dillon said. Billie raised her hand to wave at the stranger. He nodded his head curtly and turned back to the smoker.

"Thank you for coming, Cameron," she said. "I look forward to trying out what you have to offer."

Cameron nodded again but didn't turn around. Billie cast Dillon a doubtful look.

"Cam, why don't you tell Billie here a little bit about your experience?" Dillon suggested.

"Not much to tell," Cam said, still facing the grill. "I trained right out of high school, ran my own restaurant at age twenty-five, and lost everything within fifteen years."

"But that wasn't your fault," Dillon added quickly. "Your old business partner…"

"When things were going well, they went really well," Cam said suddenly. He turned around and faced Billie. "I'm happy to fill you in on everything that happened back then, but I'd be happier to show you what I can do with your food truck."

Billie smiled. "Of course. Do you have a time in mind that you will be ready with your menu? I want to make sure to be here when you're all set up and ready."

"What time is it right now?" Cam asked.

"Just after nine," Dillon offered.

"Okay," Cam said. He appeared to be thinking. "Meet me back here at noon. I'll have a feast ready and waiting for you."

"Are you okay if Asher comes also?" Billie asked.

"Who is Asher?"

"He's the other owner of the festival grounds and the commissary kitchen," Billie said.

"He's also her snuggle bunny," Dillon teased. Billie gasped at him in shock. She was surprised to see his humorous side.

"You can bring the entire village," Cam said, smiling for the first time. "Snuggle bunnies are welcome, too."

Billie responded by picking up a roll of paper towels and tossing them in the direction of the two men. She walked into the commissary kitchen, planning to clear space in the walk-in cooler, and to check to see if there was any more ice cream for her. But first she walked down the hall toward her office. She wanted to check the computer to see if the internet was still down.

Voices down the hall brought her back out of her office. She headed straight for the kitchen area and grinned as she approached Asher. He was standing a few feet from a short man wearing a tall cowboy hat.

"And who is this?" the man asked. He frowned at Billie. His eyebrows were drawn together. Billie was taken aback by his reaction to her.

"This is Billie Halifax. She is my partner here and the owner of the food truck fleet."

The man's face instantly changed. "Oh, okay," he said with a big smile. "You're the other half of this little venue. I am happy to meet you. Name's Frank

Price. I'm the head of the Ranchers Association and the sponsor of the festival you good folks are about to host."

"I'm pleased to meet you as well," Billie said. She took the man's hand and shook it. "I hear this is going to be a great event."

"It had better be. I don't have any time for it to go otherwise, and I'm sure you folks don't either."

"Okay, then." Billie attempted a smile. "I'm sure it will be wonderful."

"Alrighty," Frank said with a grin as big as the hat on his head. "You folks have quite the setup, don't you?"

"We're proud you think so. We love this little piece of paradise ourselves," Asher said in an accent Billie had never heard him use before. "Now, tell me, Mr. Price. Have you been down to the boardwalk just yet to check out the street food we have down there?"

"Oh, I am more than interested in those food trucks," Frank said. "You've properly vetted these folks, right?"

"You can come right outside and meet our barbecue truck manager if you'd like," Asher said, raising a brow. "His name is Dillon Frazier, and he is a genius." Billie was surprised at the praise. She had never heard Asher speak so fondly of any of her truck managers.

"Why don't you head outside, and we'll be right along?" Billie suggested. "Just follow that sweet smell and you will find Dillon and our newest manager, Cameron."

"I will do just that," Frank said. He tipped his hat to her and smiled.

Billie waited for him to be out of earshot and smacked Asher with the back of her hand.

"What was that for?" Asher asked, holding his stomach.

"What on earth was that performance all about? 'Have you been down to the boardwalk to check out our food trucks, Mr. Price? Welcome to our little corner of paradise, Mr. Price. And what was with the accent?"

"I don't know." He laughed. "I was trying to set the tone."

"Yeah, yeah. Whatever you say," Billie teased.

"That's why I'm the salesman around here and you are not," Asher said. "But let's talk about you. Cameron is a sure thing, then?"

"He is the best hope we have for all of the food trucks to be up and running this weekend," Billie said.

"I'm putting all of my trust into Dillon. I think he's earned it."

"I don't disagree with you there," Asher said. "Now let's get on outside so I can meet this new truck manager and make sure Frank doesn't chase him off."

"Why would you be worried about that? What's wrong with Frank?" Billie asked. She had a few hesitations of her own, but she couldn't quite put her finger on why.

CHAPTER SEVEN

Billie felt her stomach churn while she waited for Cam to serve the first sampling of his menu. She leaned over to Dillon who was seated at her left. "You're sure this guy knows what he is doing?" she whispered.

"How many times do I have to tell you he is a pro?" Dillon replied. "I told you he was a guest speaker at the culinary school about as often as I was."

"I know. I'm sorry," Billie said. "I'm just a little gun shy after the other day. I still don't know what she put in those sliders that made me sick."

Dillon patted her hand. "I get it, Billie," he said. "I really do. I'm kind of surprised you're even here right now to sample the menu. If the internet was up,

I'd show you some of the awards his restaurant won back in the day."

"If it went that well, why did it shut down?"

"It shut down because Cam trusted the wrong person," Dillon said. "It had nothing to do with the food."

Billie sat upright and watched Cam in action. He moved with more poise and precision than any of the other food truck managers during their auditions, aside from Dillon himself. She watched as he assembled the first burger on the plate. He piled ingredients on top of the burger and then placed the top bun slightly askew to showcase the ingredients.

"What is going on in here?" Alex Regent appeared at her side suddenly. Billie almost burst out laughing when she saw him. He wore a three-piece, white linen suit with a pocket watch chain dangling from the vest pocket.

"This is a food truck manager audition," Billie said. She smiled and pointed to the seat across the table from her.

"Alright, lady and gentlemen," Cam announced from the test kitchen. "Up first is my Blueberry Brie Burger," he said. He tipped a plate toward them and pointed out the ingredients as he described them.

"We start with the brisket burger topped with a

sweet blueberry compote, sweet grilled onions, tangy brie, and a pepper and garlic aioli."

Billie stood up first and headed for the serving counter. She exhaled and took one of the plates. She waited for the others to get their plates, then took a cautious bite. A variety of flavors exploded in her mouth. First was the unmistakable sweet and smoky flavor from the burger itself followed by the sweetness of the berries and the tartness of the cheese. "Oh, that is just incredible," she said, taking a second bite.

"Asher?" Dillon waited for him to take a bite.

"Can't talk now," Asher said with his mouth full. "I'm a little busy here with the best burger I have ever eaten."

"So, this is how things work?" Alex asked. He took a bite of his burger then. "Oh, wow. I need to show up every time you have one of these auditions."

"I think the first burger is a resounding success, Cam," Dillon said to his friend. Cam nodded, barely smiling. Billie was quickly learning that was a sign of his approval of the situation.

"Let's move on, then," he said. He followed the blueberry and brie burger with a bacon, lettuce, and tomato version. Once again, Billie was astounded. Next he offered his "Caliente Burger," a half-pound patty infused with garlic and jalapeño pepper juice and topped with smoked cheddar cheese, Carolina-style slaw, and bread and butter pickles.

"Last up, I have two more sandwiches to share with you," Cam announced. "First is what I call The Basic. This is a simple burger, something you would expect from a backyard cookout, but the patty itself is extraordinary. I've included my signature ground smoked brisket mixed with ground sirloin and a few secret ingredients in the burger. Toppings are your choice. I encourage you to try the bacon cheeseburger version."

Billie bit into the burger and smiled. "Brown sugar, butter, and red onions," she said.

"Very good," Cam said. He smiled fully for the first time. "Add a few more surprises and you have just about figured out the secret recipe."

"Billie isn't too keen on secret ingredients these days," Asher said with a chuckle.

"Are you the one who was poisoned by the other girl?" Cam asked suddenly.

Billie nodded her head. "That would be me," she said. "At least, that's what we think."

"Then I am beyond impressed that you showed up here today to sample what I have to offer," he said. "I don't know if I could have ever tried a burger again."

"Well, it's my job to taste test everything that comes from one of my food trucks," Billie said. "That and the recommendation you got from this big guy here was all I needed to know." She jerked her thumb toward Dillon.

"Thanks. I think," Dillon replied.

"What do you have last?" Alex asked. He was getting into the taste-testing process. The lapel of his white suit coat was streaked with barbecue sauce and other signs of his enthusiasm.

"Thank you for asking, Mr. Regent," Cam said. He sounded more reassured the longer he spoke. "My last offering is what I like to call a grown up grilled cheese." He set a large sandwich on each plate. "I start with this thick sliced Texas toast perfectly grilled in butter on the griddle. Inside you will find four smoked cheeses. I have included cheddar, Swiss, gouda, and mozzarella along with spinach and arugula, more of the garlic and pepper aioli over a layer of loose meat."

"Loose meat?" Billie asked.

Cam nodded. "It's the same thing you will find in the burger patties, but in loose form," he explained. "The loose meat is simply chopped and browned with onion and seasonings instead of a patty. It works much better in this sandwich."

Billie took a bite and closed her eyes. "That is perfect," she said.

"I want mine with a steaming bowl of chili," Asher said.

Dillon smiled and smacked the counter with his hand. "I told you, Cam," he said. "We were just talking about working on that together. When the rainy season is here, you pair that grilled cheese with some chili, and we'll have to beat back the crowds."

"I'm shocked you don't have to do that already," Alex said. He pulled a linen handkerchief out of his shirt pocket and dabbed his mouth with it. Billie looked at his plate. Half of the grilled cheese was already gone.

"What have we got going on in here?" Frank asked from the other side of the kitchen space. "And why wasn't I invited?"

"This is an audition," Alex announced with glee. Asher cast a worried look at Billie.

"An audition?" Frank asked with a frown. "Who all is here and what do they want?"

"Yes, this is the new food truck manager, and he's here to share his menu with all of us," Alex continued.

"Would you like to try the best burger you have ever eaten?"

"Asher, Billie, can I see you for a second?" Frank asked. He headed down the hallway to Asher's office. "Now."

Billie followed Asher down the hall. She was beyond irritated at the short, squat cowboy, but she had to watch her tongue. The last thing she needed was to spout off at the man and get the festival canceled, especially when she planned to debut the burger truck at the event.

"What's going on, Frank?" Asher asked. Billie noted he had moved beyond "Mr. Price."

"What's going on is the two of you reassured me that everything was in place for this weekend," he said. "You can't go on and hire someone willy nilly like that. Not before one of my events. You never know who is going to show up."

"That's not how things go around here. I promise we know what we're doing," Billie said, not so sure of the words.

Frank crossed his arms. "I don't care what you say. This is my event and I want things done properly. Hiring a new manager in the middle of my event isn't smart. Believe me when I say, you can't trust folks nowadays. Not only that, but I also have to find out that you don't already have a staff in place. A new cook? Are you prepared for my event or not?"

"Mr. Price, you've heard about the events that took place on the mainland with the young woman's body discovered at the bus station, right?" Billie began.

"Yes, yes," Frank said. He waved his hands around. "What does that have to do with anything?"

"It has a lot to do with everything," Billie said, deciding that honesty was the best policy. "We have a bit of a mystery on our hands. The woman who was found dead may have something to do with why I got sick. I think she came here claiming to be someone else, the original manager I hired. I also think that she fed me something that wasn't okay, and it resulted in a case of food poisoning." As she revealed her suspicions, she tried hard to ignore the look on Asher's face.

"Food poisoning? Are you kidding me?" Frank asked. "You two are just digging your own graves deeper and deeper."

"Mr. Shields is here as a replacement, and he comes highly recommended," Asher said.

"He does, does he?" Frank smirked. "How do you know this guy can create anything decent on a grill?"

"Well, if you had shut your mouth long enough to hear what we have been trying to tell you, the answer would have been apparent," Asher said. Billie turned to him in shock.

"I'll thank you to remember who you are talking to, boy," Frank sneered.

"And I will thank you to remember that this is a place of business and you and I are both business-men," Asher returned. "I am not a boy nor am I a novice in this business. I've successfully run these festival grounds for more than a decade. I do know what I am doing, Mr. Price. If you have doubts, then you can easily pull out of our contract, but you will pay the termination fee. This is not the corral on one of your ranches and we are not livestock. I expect decency and manners from anyone I do business with."

"Well, then," Frank said. He cleared his throat a few times. "I guess you feel better about yourself now. I have too much to lose to cancel this weekend, so let's just hope that this new guy is as good as you seem to think he is." He jerked his head at Billie and headed toward the door. When he reached the door, he hesitated while a man dressed in a green uniform stepped inside.

"I'm looking for Billie Halifax and Asher Jenk-ins," the man said.

"And who are you?" Frank demanded.

"Ken Avery. Sheriff Ken Avery," he said. "I just have a few questions."

"Oh, now that is just wonderful," Frank said. He pointed at Asher. "You better deliver, boy. Or I will make you eat your words."

"Who was that?" the sheriff asked.

"Frank Price," Asher answered. "He's the man who might be capable of putting me out of business."

CHAPTER EIGHT

"What does the sheriff want?" Alex leaned over and whispered to Billie. She responded with the shrug of her shoulders. Asher was in the office speaking with him at that very moment.

"I imagine he wants to ask us what we know about everything that's been going on." She felt her stomach churn as she said the words.

"Well, he needs to listen to me," Alex said. "I wonder if he's spoken to the chief yet?"

"You know, I think I'm going to give Cam a tour of the food truck when he is finished cleaning up," Dillon suggested.

Billie smiled. "You absolutely should," she said. "In fact, why don't you run down to my office and grab the folder off of my desk with his contract in it. I trust you to go over things with him. The truck keys are on my desk as well. You could take him to the boardwalk and show him around. Introduce him to everyone."

"Oh, I think I will go with you," Alex said.

"No, Alex," Billie said. "I think you are going to be needed here. You're right. You do have something to say to the sheriff. I'm sure he's already talked to the chief, but this is important."

"Right." Alex nodded his head. "I was just saying that myself, wasn't I? It's a symptom of entering your eighth decade."

Billie smiled and nodded to Dillon. "You're my head manager, Dillon," she said. "If you don't mind orienting your friend to the business, I'd really appreciate it. I'll check in and sign the contract myself the second I'm free."

Dillon nodded at her and beamed. "I am grateful for your confidence in me," he said. He looked up at Cam who had just emerged from the test kitchen. "Come on, old pal. Let's get things set up for you." They walked together down the other side of the building toward Billie's office.

Billie breathed a sigh of relief when they had gone. It was enough to worry about Frank and what he had to say about things, let alone scaring off the best hope she had for the burger truck at the same time.

"What do you think of Cam?" Alex asked her when the two men headed outside.

"I hope this mess with Julie, or whoever she was, doesn't scare him off," she said. "I want him in my fleet."

"He knows his way around the kitchen," Alex said.

"That he does," Billie said. "But that isn't the only reason why. He is an older man, and he has been through some loss. You can tell that."

"Why does that make any difference to you?" Alex asked.

She searched his face. His question seemed sincere. "Because he has a reason to be here, and he knows how to handle himself behind the counter, I believe," she said. "When I first started this business after my grandmother died, I had the idea that I would give anything to go back to my early twenties and start over. But I've since learned that not everyone older than twenty-two is ruined. Sometimes an older person with experience makes the best candidate for this job."

"Like Dillon?"

"Exactly like Dillon," Billie said. "He is a gem,

Alex. I love the passion and youth many of the others have brought to the table with them, but Dillon is a grounding force here. That's why he is my right hand man."

"Asher isn't?" Alex asked.

Billie nodded her head. "Asher is my rock for other reasons," she said. "Like how he handled Frank just now."

"Miss Halifax?" Sheriff Avery appeared just then. "May I speak with you now?"

"You need to speak with me as well, Sheriff," Alex stepped forward and said.

"Who are you?" the sheriff asked.

"Alex Regent. I am this young woman's attorney," Alex said. "I'm also the man who arranged for a young woman named Julie Neilson to come out here in the first place. And I can tell you the young woman who came out here and claimed to be her was not her."

"And how do you know that?" the sheriff asked.

"Because I left her on the mainland," Alex said. "She appeared at the culinary school and announced that she did not want to move to out this way after all. This happened after Billie met with whoever that was and got sick."

"Is that what happened, to your knowledge?" Sheriff Avery asked Billie.

"Yes," she said. "I was shocked when I found out that the girl that was here wasn't Julie. I have no idea who she was, and it disturbs me that I got sick from what she made."

"What happened when you got sick?" the sheriff asked her.

"Are you asking me about my symptoms, because I would rather not share those details with you, sir."

"No, that's not what I am asking," the sheriff said. "Where were you when you got sick?"

"I was on Asher's houseboat at the marina," she said.

"Are you and Mr. Scanlan a couple, Miss Halifax?"

Billie nodded her head. "Yes sir, we are," she said. "He insisted on taking me to the urgent care clinic when I was sick."

"Can you prove that?" the sheriff asked.

"I can," she said. "I have the paperwork from the clinic and a receipt from the pharmacy afterward."

"Where did you go after you visited the clinic and filled your prescriptions?" the sheriff asked her.

"Back to my house," she said. "And it was only one prescription."

"Okay, and where do you live?" Sheriff Avery asked.

"Did you happen to see the fifth wheel when you arrived? Over on the far side of the grounds where the gate leads to the beach?"

The sheriff nodded. "I saw the RV and another building of sorts," he said.

"Well, that other building is where I live," Billie said. "It's a tiny house."

"What did you do when you got home?" he asked her.

"I slept for like two days and felt much better when I woke up," she said.

"Where was Mr. Scanlan during that time?"

"At my house with me," she said. "He was there when I went to sleep and there when I woke up. He was also there anytime I woke up to use the bathroom."

"Can anyone else verify that?" the sheriff asked.

Billie nodded. "One of my managers lives in the fifth wheel," she said. "Her name is Polly Sheridan. She runs the ice cream truck down on the boardwalk with her twin sister, Liza."

The sheriff nodded. "One last question," he said. He pulled a cell phone out of his pocket and turned the screen toward her. "Do you recognize this woman?"

Billie stared at the photo for a brief second. "Yes! That's the woman who identified herself as Julie Neilson," she said. "She is the one who was here and cooked for me. She is the one who made me sick."

Sheriff Avery turned the phone screen off and nodded his head. "That's exactly what Asher said as well."

"I can tell you unequivocally that is not Julie Neilson," Alex said. "I interviewed her for Billie and have seen her several times at the culinary school. That is not her."

"I am aware of that now, Mr. Regent," the sheriff said. "That photo is of a woman named Tara Trent. She is a missing person from Glenford, Texas."

"Who is she and why was she pretending to be Julie Neilson?" Billie asked.

Sheriff Avery shook his head. "If we knew that, we might know who killed her," he said.

CHAPTER NINE

"I wish the cell towers would come back up," Billie complained. "I don't know how I ever lived my life without the internet or texting."

"You could go to the mainland and stop in at a fast food place or something. I'm sure they have internet there you can hook up to."

"You know I can't drive to the mainland," Billie said.

"I know you won't drive to the mainland," Asher said, "I don't believe you are incapable of doing it."

Billie ignored his teasing and checked her cell phone again. "Oh, you know what? I do have signal!"

"Jeez. Is there an important phone call you are wanting to make or something?" Asher asked her.

Billie shook her head. "No, but I've been very

interested in finding out as much as I can about this Tara person since the sheriff showed us her picture." She began typing into the search engine. "I want to find out more about this young woman who showed up here pretending to be one of the students from the culinary school. I still wonder if she lost out on the job or something and got mad."

"I haven't got a clue," Asher said. "I'm just happy that the sheriff seemed to take us at our word about where we were. He didn't have to do that."

Billie nodded her head slowly. "Trust me when I tell you I've been thinking about that since he left," she said. "I assume they know more then they're letting on though, and there's no reason for him to think we had anything to do with it."

"Why are you so curious about this girl? Why not just let the cops do their jobs this time?" Asher asked her.

Billie tried to suppress her annoyance with him. She had a million reasons for checking into the woman who likely poisoned her. The least of which was finding out a reason why. "I have a real interest in finding out more about the person who deliberately fed me something that made me sick," she said.

Asher left it alone after that. He announced that he was going to head back to his own office and check on the smaller vendors scheduled to arrive first thing in the morning for the festival, now that the internet and cell service had been restored.

Billie searched Tara Trent's name as soon as he left her office. Mostly everything she found was about two women in the Fort Myers area, both of whom were part of the same quilting collective. She also found a yoga teacher in the Miami area with the same name, but no one even remotely close in age to the woman who had come to the commissary kitchen purporting to be Julie Neilson.

She began to wonder if the name of the woman was even correct. Could she have been working under a fake name once again? Billie cleared her search again and sat back in her chair and thought. Sheriff Avery had said that Tara was a missing woman from Texas. A quick search of newspapers brought up an article about the missing young woman. She read that article and another two that showed her photo. Clearly it was the same girl, but why would she take on the name of another woman from a different state and travel all the way to Florida pretending to be her?

Maybe the real Julie Neilson could shed some light on the situation. Billie opened her email account and found the exchange between herself and the young chef before she had apparently decided not to come out to Sea Glass Island. For one reason or another, mostly schedule related, Billie had not been able to set up a video conference with this food truck candidate as she had most of the others. She had no idea if the young woman would agree to talk with her or not, but she sent a short email requesting a video chat.

To her surprise, Julie answered right away. "I'm not sure why you want to chat with me at this point, but sure," she replied.

Billie wasted no time setting up the video call. She sent the request without replying to the email and waited while Julie answered the call.

"Billie?"

"That's me," Billie said, smiling into the camera. "You must be Julie. The real Julie Neilson."

"That I am," Julie said. She still hadn't smiled. "You will have to forgive me, but why are you reaching out to me now?"

Billie sighed. She had not thought through the conversation. "I'll admit that I am just winging it right now, but I wanted to see if you could maybe help me figure out a few things," she said.

"If you're going to grill me over why I decided not to come out for the job interview, I really have nothing to say," Julie said.

Billie shrugged her shoulders. "I am curious about that, but not for the reasons you probably think," she said.

"And what reasons would those be?" Julie asked. She was clearly irritated already.

"Well, I imagine you're sitting there thinking that I am going to demand a reason or an explanation," Billie said. "But that's not really it at all."

"Okay, then what is it?" Julie's features softened.

"I'm curious about what happened just before you decided not to come, but only because I am trying to figure out this other woman and why she pretended to be you," Billie said.

"You do know that I have already been grilled by the police about this, right?"

Billie shook her head. "I can only imagine that you have," Billie said. "But they haven't told me a thing that answers my questions."

"What are your questions? Why would I back out of the chance of a lifetime? Why I chose to stay and be closer to my family?" Julie's voice grew louder as she spoke.

"No, no," Billie said, shaking her head. "It's more or less trying everything I can to figure out why this woman pretending to be you deliberately made me sick."

Julie sat back a little in her chair. Her face registered shock, although Billie had no idea if it was sincere. "What do you mean, she made you sick?"

"Exactly what I just said," Billie replied. "When you and I were corresponding back and forth, I explained how I would make time for you to come to the commissary kitchen and create a sampling of your menu, and what you envisioned for the food truck. Do you remember that?"

Julie nodded her head. "I do recall that," she said. "Believe it or not, I had actually started my menu as soon as you emailed me about that."

"This other woman, whoever she really is, showed up and created three small sliders with the promise that she would return later that day to finish her audition," she explained. "I ate the sliders. I always eat what the new managers serve. This woman left almost immediately after she plated the food. I didn't detect anything at first, but I was deathly ill two hours later."

"She poisoned you?"

"That's what I'm trying to say," Billie said. "Julie, you have your reasons for not coming out here and I don't hold that against you whatsoever."

"Okay, but I still don't know what I can tell you that will help you," Julie said.

"Well, I was just wondering if anyone approached

you or threatened you in any way," Billie said. "The one thing I cannot begin to understand is how this Tara person even knew anything about you or me or this place at all. I was wondering if maybe someone from the school was upset that you were chosen over them?"

Julie shook her head. "I really don't want to keep talking about this. I'm sorry I can't take the job, and I'm sorry I wasted your time. I have to go." She abruptly ended the call. Billie stared at the blank screen for a moment before it dawned on her that Julie had cut off the call.

CHAPTER TEN

Billie was still a little dumbfounded from the conversation with Julie and the sudden end to it. Deciding she needed to clear her head, she attached Waffles to his leash and tucked her phone into her back pocket.

She was grateful that the sun was hidden behind the clouds as they hit the beach and headed toward the water. They went all the way to the dog beach where she unhooked the leash and set Waffles free to play in the water. Billie stood back and watched him with a smile on her face. His antics helped her clear her mind a bit. For days she had felt like she had been doing nothing but reacting to one thing after another. It was time to get creative.

At first, she had considered the idea of reaching

out to the real Julie a creative answer. The only problem was that she had not come up with any worthwhile answers. Her search for Tara hadn't been all that helpful, and the police were not very forthcoming with information. And despite the fact that he was on the island for the first time in a long time, Alex Regent was not helpful at all.

A thought hit her. She should follow up with Julie, even if it was a fruitless effort. Giving her a better reason to trust her might work in her favor. She pulled out her phone and opened her email once again. She typed out a fast message to Julie, thanking her for taking the time to meet with her and apologizing for her scatter-brained questions. She reiterated her questions about the reasons the stranger had chosen to use Julie's identity and then use it to harm her. She ended the email by admitting that she was scared.

If the email would make any difference to Julie, Billie had no idea. She just wanted to reach out and explain herself a little bit more. She turned her attention back to Waffles. His whines suddenly filled the air. She raced toward him and found him with a golden-colored crab attached to his snout by a large claw.

"Oh, Waffles! How in the world did you get yourself into this situation?" She reattached the leash to his collar and forced him to stay in one place.

"Is everything okay?" Detective Sullivan's voice called across the beach to her.

Billie looked up and shook her head. "I think he messed with the wrong crab," Billie said.

Sully raced toward them. "You really have gotten yourself into a mess here," she said to Waffles.

"Do you know what to do?" Billie asked her.

"Hold his head still if you can," Sully instructed. Billie dropped to the sand on her knees. She tucked the leash under one knee and wrapped her arms around the dog's head. Sully worked without talking. She reached inside her pocket and produced a pocket knife. Billie held the dog as still as she could while the detective worked.

Sully opened the knife and inserted the blade carefully into the claw. She pressed down and held on until the crab released the poor dog's snout. The crab fell to the beach and skittered off toward the water.

Waffles looked up at Billie. He whimpered and slumped down to the sand.

"Poor baby," Sully said. "I bet he's going to be feeling that for a week."

"Do you think I need to take him to the vet?"

Billie cradled the dog's face in her hands and examined his nose and mouth.

Sully crouched down next to her. "I don't think so," she said. "I've been a dog mom for twenty-five years. I don't see an open wound. If he isn't better in a few days, you might want to take him in. For now, just take him home. Give him soft foods and maybe something frozen to work on."

"I can do that," Billie said.

"Do you want me to walk with you?"

Billie looked up at the detective and smiled. "Sure," she said. "I could use the company." She pulled up gently on the leash to encourage Waffles to his feet. The dog walked along slowly. Gone was his typical bounding energy.

"Did you speak with Sheriff Avery?" Sully asked her. "The chief said he was on the island."

Billie nodded. She looked ahead as she spoke, not wanting to seem as desperate as she felt for information from the detective. "I did speak with him," she said. "Asher did, too. This whole situation is crazy."

"Did he tell you anything interesting?" Sully asked.

"Well, he showed me the photo of a missing young woman," Billie said. "Her name is Tara Trent, and she was the woman who came claiming to be Julie Neilson."

"I heard about that," Sully said. "Were you able to confirm her identity?"

"I was able to recognize her as the same person, yes," Billie said. "So many things about this just don't make a bit of sense."

"Like why she was here pretending to be a person she possibly never even met?"

Billie nodded. "I spoke with the real Julie a little while ago, over video chat," she said. "I thought she might have some information to make it all make sense."

Sully stopped walking. "And did she?"

Billie shook her head again. "Nothing," she said. "I think she was more concerned with the reasons I reached out than she was with this whole mystery surrounding the other young woman."

"Can I ask you something?" Sully said.

"Of course," Billie answered.

"What did you hope Julie would be able to tell you when you spoke to her?" Sully asked. "What were you looking for exactly?"

"A reason," Billie said. "Like, maybe there was a mysterious young woman who threatened her and forced her to stay where she was."

"And decided to come to the same place Julie was supposed to go and then pretended to be her just so she would make you, a total stranger, sick?"

"Pretty far-fetched, isn't it?" Billie said.

"To say the least," Sully agreed. "I'll admit that this is a really weird situation, though."

Billie walked several more feet before speaking up again. "Is there anything that you know about the investigation that you can tell me? Like, do they have a motive or a suspect yet?"

Sully shook her head. "They've figured out that she was strangled and dropped off at the bus station," she said. "They don't know why she was dropped off there or anything more. Or at least nothing they are telling me or anyone else."

"No description to go on or a car or anything?"

"Not a thing," Sully said. "The chief seems to think the suspect was probably not from the island. He thinks she was killed by someone who was connected to the mainland."

"Do you know what makes him think so?"

"Just a lack of evidence from the island, I guess. No sand at the crime scene." She forced an awkward laugh. Sully hesitated long enough to open the gate to the festival grounds. "You know, there's something I have been meaning to ask you."

Billie's throat tightened a bit. She was still unsure if she could trust the detective, or if her friendliness was an act to throw her off guard. "What's that?"

"When you spoke with the woman who came to see you," Sully began. "Did she ever say she was Julie Neilson? Or did you ask her if she was?"

Billie stopped walking. She held onto the fence post and stared at the detective. "I don't know," she said. Her mind raced to remember. "I thought she had said she was Julie."

"Maybe you asked her if she was Julie and she either said she was or she didn't deny it," Sully said. "But do you remember clearly if she came up to you and introduced herself as Julie?"

Billie closed her eyes for a moment and pictured the interaction with the young woman at the commissary kitchen. Julie, or who she had thought was Julie, had come inside and was standing in the hallway near the women's restroom when Billie approached her. She responded when Billie spoke to her.

"No," she said suddenly. "She was just standing there when I came out of my office. I must have just assumed she was Julie."

"Did she have anything with her? Cooking utensils, a cookbook, that sort of thing?"

Billie shook her head. "Nope. She came with

nothing, which I thought was a little odd, but I figured maybe I wasn't clear enough about my expectations. I find it easier to assume that I did something wrong, than to think someone else messed up." She frowned. "Anyway, I led her back to the pantry and showed her where the cooler was."

"And she cooked for you? Is it normal for them to show up empty handed?"

"No, but again, it's possible that it was my fault. I didn't get to have the typical interviews with her to explain everything. We kept having a hard time getting in touch."

"Was her food good? I mean, did she know her way around the kitchen?" Sully asked.

"The food was okay. Billie laughed. "But she seemed a little… I don't know nervous or intimidated or something."

"I hate to say this, but that should have been the first thing to set you off. You never found out if it was really her, she didn't bring anything with her, and she didn't seem to be a pro in the kitchen. I don't know if it's a helpful clue now, but it should have been before."

Billie knew the detective was right. She should have caught this much sooner.

CHAPTER ELEVEN

The detective continued down the beach in the direction of the boardwalk. Billie secured Waffles back in his pen and waved to Sully. Her freezer lacked much to help the poor pooch forget his fight with the crab. She decided to simply offer a bowl of ice water and a can of soft dog food and head back to the commissary kitchen in search of something that might be more appropriate.

A few vendors had begun to arrive for the festival. Billie spotted Cam in the brand new burger truck. She looked around for Dillon but didn't see him. He had likely returned to his own food truck. It was close to dinner time, and it would be all hands on deck for the rush down on the boardwalk.

Billie forced herself to think more clearly about

her interaction with Tara, the woman she had confused for Julie. Sully's questions made more sense to her than the assumption that Tara had pretended to be Julie. It was also a good explanation for why Julie herself didn't have any answers. Billie was beginning to wonder how much of this was her fault. If she had actually made sure that the person she was talking to was Julie, maybe none of this would have ever happened. However, there was no reason she could think of that someone would want to poison her. She needed to check with Alex to see if Tara had been a student at the culinary school, but even if she had wanted to get the real Julie out of the way, why would she have poisoned her on purpose, and who would have killed her?

Billie sighed. Maybe it was just dumb luck. The entire interaction could have been a coincidence. It was still possible poisoning wasn't intentional. So far, there was no proof that Tara had actually meant her any harm. She might have inadvertently caused her illness simply by not knowing what in the heck she was doing. Her thoughts went back to the culinary school. There was almost no way a trained chef wouldn't have been able to detect if the meat was off or something wasn't cooked thoroughly. The likelihood of Tara wanting to steal Julie's job was pretty slim.

She let herself into the commissary kitchen building and headed straight for the cooler. Dillon and some of the other cooks were known to keep bones and scraps for Waffles, which the spoiled pooch greatly appreciated. She was counting on a frozen bone to help the dog out.

Maybe Tara actually served her some of the meat that was meant for the dog. It could be that one of the cooks had set aside meat that was a little past its expiration date for humans and the girl was unaware and decided to make a slider out of it. Even if she had, there was one glaring question that would not answer. Why was Tara pretending to be Julie in the first place? Billie wanted to reach out to Julie again and get out of her if there was more she wasn't telling her about her decision not to come out for the job.

Her phone rang in her pocket.

"Hello, this is Billie," she said, leaving the cooler.

"Billie, this is Dr. Hughes, from the clinic. I believe you visited our urgent care a few days ago with complaints of abdominal distress, suspected food poisoning?"

"Yes," Billie said. "I saw the nurse practitioner."

"And she drew some blood, is that right?" Dr. Hughes asked her.

"That's right," she said. "I think she wanted to test to make sure what was actually making me sick."

"She did, and she prescribed some antibiotics, right?"

"She did, and I am feeling much better," Billie said.

"What sort of food did you eat before you started feeling sick? Were you eating pizza, for example," he asked.

"No. I ate three small hamburgers," Billie said. "Sliders. They were prepared for me by someone I thought was trying out to be the manager of a street food truck."

"Okay, did any of these burgers have special ingredients, like maybe grilled onions or mushrooms?"

"No, no," Billie said. "They were fairly plain. Standard condiments."

"I do have some results for you, but first I need to ask you if you have any food allergies or sensitivities?" he asked.

"None that I know of," Billie said, slightly confused at the question. "Why do you need to know that?"

"Well, because the results I have here are pretty interesting," Dr. Hughes said. "Billie, you did not have any of the typical food poisoning bacteria. No salmonella, e coli, listeria, and so on."

"I didn't? None of the blood tests were positive?"

"Not like you'd think, but one blood test did show a high level of substances that are common after ingesting toxic mushrooms," he said. "Now there is no way to know now unless you still have a sample of the food you consumed somewhere, but I feel confident saying that mushroom poisoning is highly suspected. And in order for it to be this amount, I would say you had to have been aware of the mushrooms on these sliders."

"But there were no mushrooms on the burgers," Billie said.

"Well, then I'm afraid to say that, based on the levels, it really sounds like the poisoning was deliberate," Dr. Hughes said. "The good news is you overcame it and that is about the best we can hope for in a case like this. You were given a toxic dose, but not a fatal dose."

"Oh, my gosh," Billie said.

"I would like for you to come back into the clinic on Monday so I can pull some more blood and just double check to make sure your liver is still functioning as it should," he continued. "Can you call back and make an appointment for that for a time that works for you?"

"Sure," Billie said absently. "I just don't understand why someone would do that." She thanked the doctor and hung up her phone. For a moment, she paced around the kitchen space in reflection. She had been poisoned, and not by bad meat or subpar cooking practices. Someone had given her a dose, though not fatal, of a poisonous mushroom.

Billie knew enough from her years in the kitchen and her training at the culinary school, that a number of things could be put into ground meat of any kind and remain fairly undetectable. The picture was clearer to her now. Tara Trent had come into her path and pretended to be someone else, and then deliberately prepared something that made her sick. Just why and how she had done it escaped her. So did the reasons anyone else would want to kill the woman.

CHAPTER TWELVE

The mood around the island was buzzing the following morning, despite the larger than normal police presence around the festival grounds. Billie spotted Detective Sullivan, Chief Abernathy, and Sheriff Avery within the time it took her to walk from her tiny house over to the commissary kitchen building. Her plan was to visit with each of her food truck managers before they opened their doors. Since it was a festival, each of the trucks had left the normal spot on the boardwalk and parked in a prime vendor space for the next three days.

The trucks would also open up sooner than usual due to the nine o'clock start time of the festival. Billie could hear the din of voices and cooking activity the second she entered the metal building. With the exception of the Sheridan twins and Enid Greene, the kitchen space was filled with bustling managers and a dizzying variety of delicious aromas. Both of the dessert themed food trucks had been prepared for first thing that morning, long before Billie wanted to get up out of bed.

"How is Waffles this morning?" Asher asked her the second he got close enough to her. "I felt so bad when I stopped over and saw him last night."

"He's doing okay but was unwilling to go on a walk along the beach this morning," Billie said.

The truth was, she wasn't too keen to go for a walk herself. The weight of the past few days rested heavily on her. She stood back next to one of the tables in the seating area and watched her managers work around each other. There was a good deal of good-natured joking around going on, even with the presence of her newest manager, Cam. Billie watched as Isa Carello tossed a wad of raw pizza dough at Dillon, who then deflected the dough toward Cam. The dough landed squarely on his shoulder leaving a white stain behind when he pulled it off and tossed it in the garbage. He turned his back to the rest of them for a moment, concentrating at the sink in his test kitchen before emerging with the sprayer, grinning wildly and showering Isa and Dillon with cold water for their trouble.

Despite her heavy mood, Billie chuckled. There was something thrilling to her about watching her employees come together. She turned back to Asher. "I'm going to take care of a few things in my office," she said. "Have you seen Alex this morning? Or Frank?"

Asher shook his head. "I'm not shocked that Alex is a little busy. He mentioned getting breakfast with Rhonda this morning. I think they'll be here in a little while. And as far as Frank goes, I don't think we will see much of him until later on today. I'm sure he'll be too busy to bother with us."

Billie nodded her head. She kissed him briefly on the cheek and headed down the hallway to her office. She closed the door behind her and opened her laptop. Since hanging up the phone with the doctor, her curiosity had soared. She wanted to find out all she could about toxic mushrooms and what they might have done to her body. At first, she had forced herself to hold off searching, but the questions invaded her thoughts so much now that she knew there would be no peace until she had more answers. She'd yet to share with anyone what the doctor had told her and wanted to get through at least the first day of the festival before she did.

For the first few minutes of her search, Billie instantly regretted opening the can of worms that appeared on her screen. The sheer number of potentially poisonous mushrooms blew her mind. She read about some cases where the fatality rate was so high it made her head spin, but she also read about cases where the symptoms were similar to her own, and typically resolved within a day. Or ended in death. The outcome was determined merely by whether the symptoms caused respiratory failure or not.

When she had enough of searching the potential fate she had escaped, Billie thought for another moment. She opened up a second window and typed in several combinations of "why would someone poison me." She added "poisoning by mushrooms" and other terms until she found something that forced her to stand straight up behind her desk, almost knocking over her office chair in the process. Maybe there was more to Tara Trent than she'd thought.

"Hey, Billie?" She heard the knock on her door and fixed her chair before responding.

"Come in," she said. Isa appeared in her doorway. Her face was tight and drawn.

"I have a little bit of an issue," she said. "The

fresh mozzarella I ordered from the food vendor is a little less than fresh. Fourteen bags exploded in the cooler overnight and there is a very evident layer of mold on most of them."

"Oh, wow," Billie said. She pinched the skin at the top of her nose. "What do you need for me to do?" She hoped the answer wasn't running across the causeway to the mainland to replace it.

"I need you to run to the mainland and replace the mozzarella for me as quickly as possible," Isa said. "I know how you feel about driving over the bridge, but I really need this."

Billie waved her hand in the air. "Oh, don't you worry about that right now," she said. "Give me a list and I will be on my way in twenty minutes." She smiled and waited for Isa to leave her office before she picked up her cell phone and panic-dialed Rhonda.

"What do you need and when do you need to go?" Rhonda did not even answer the phone call with a "hello."

"Fresh mozzarella cheese and right now," Billie said. "We can take my car."

"I've got coverage at work. We can take mine and I'll be there in five minutes," Rhonda said before she hung up the phone.

Billie pushed the phone into her back pocket and walked out to the kitchen space. She motioned for Asher to come close to her. "I have to run off the island," she said. "Isa's fresh mozzarella is rotten."

"Tell Rhonda I said hello," Asher said with a wink. He leaned down to kiss her quickly. "I'll be hanging out here with Frank. I apparently spoke too soon when I said we wouldn't see him. He won't leave me alone. He's so focused on everything going off without a hitch."

"Good luck." Billie turned toward the hallway. She wanted to be outside when Rhonda showed up. It was the least she could do for the woman who had become both her faithful taxi service and her dear friend.

"You headed somewhere?" Detective Sullivan approached her. Her face was red from the trek across the sand.

"The mainland," Billie said. "One of my managers discovered some rotten cheese."

"Oh, that's no good," Sully said. "I bet that's a pain on the first day of a festival."

"Yeah," Billie said. "Can I ask you something?"

"Of course," Sully said. "What's up?"

Billie looked around at the uniformed officers.

"This increased police presence, is that so folks feel safer about the murder on the mainland?"

Sully shook her head. "It's more to see if anything shakes out as far as the investigation itself. The public hasn't been told about the connection to the festival," she said. "And the investigation isn't going anywhere at the moment."

Rhonda pulled up and beeped her horn. Billie wanted to tell her right then about the poisoning, but really had to help Isa. "Thank you, Sully," she said. "I'll be back soon, and we can talk more."

"Is that the new detective?" Rhonda asked her the second she shut the door.

"Yes," Billie said. "That's Sully."

"Sully? That's an interesting name."

"Short for Sullivan, her last name," Billie said. "She seems nice enough."

"I guess that's a good thing," Rhonda said. She was quiet for a moment, then reached her hand over and smacked Billie on her leg. "What's up, buttercup?"

"What do you mean?" Billie asked.

"You are agitated, and preoccupied," Rhonda said. "What gives?"

Billie said. "I had a phone call from Dr. Hughes at the urgent care clinic."

"Why did he call you?" Rhonda asked.

"Blood test results," Billie said.

"Did they find anything?"

"Nothing you would think," she said. "No salmonella, no bacteria. He said I had high levels of another substance in my blood."

"Did he tell you what that meant? Does he know what made you sick?" Rhonda asked.

"He said it was most likely mushroom poisoning," Billie said.

"What? Mushroom poisoning!" Rhonda said. "Are you sure it wasn't an accident?"

Billie shook her head. "Dr. Hughes said that the levels were low enough that it had to be deliberate," she said. "If it was accidental, I would have likely had a lethal amount of it."

"And the food that girl fixed you," Rhonda said. "She didn't tell you it had mushrooms in it?"

Billie shook her head. "There were no mushrooms, Rhonda," she said. "I know how to detect the taste of them and there were none."

"But what reason would there be for that?" Rhonda asked.

"That's the question," Billie said. "There are just a few things I am unclear about right now, but something I found online points to Tara. I don't think she had a reason to hurt me specifically, I think it just sort of worked out that way."

"What does that even mean?"

"It means, I think Tara was in the right place at the wrong time. But I think I was in the wrong place at the wrong time."

CHAPTER THIRTEEN

Isa raised her hands above her as if she was praying
when Billie and Rhonda returned to the commissary
kitchen a short time later. Billie's mind turned in all
directions while she went through the motions of
helping her move her ingredients to the fridge in her
food truck. Already the people had begun to gather
around the trucks outside. She was pleased to see
Cam smiling and greeting customers from his open
window while he worked.

"When did you get back?" Asher asked her when
he caught up to her.

"Just a moment ago," Billie said. "Where are you
going?"

"Up to the main street where they have set up

their grandstand," Asher said. "Frank is about to give some welcoming speech."

Billie followed him over and waited. Frank appeared on the portable stage. He waved to several people seated on barstools across the back of the stage. He made his way to the microphone and tapped it with his finger.

"Is this thing on?" he asked. The crowd chuckled respectfully.

Billie looked to her left. Sully had made her way through the crowd. She glanced around. Sheriff Avery wasn't far off, and Chief Abernathy stood to the side of the stage with his arms folded over his wide chest.

"I want to welcome all of you here to this beautiful setting for the seventy-ninth annual gathering of this fine group," Frank said. "We are the results of a proud tradition of farmers and ranchers, beef producers, and suppliers who follow the pattern set for us by our forefathers." His voice rose as he spoke.

"And like nearly every year, there are those who try to stop our efforts," Frank continued. "But we will always prevail over our enemies. We are gathered here and now to celebrate the great traditions we represent and the service we give to this great nation of ours. We feed America! Good, old fashioned

American beef!" He raised both arms over his head and beamed in the applause.

Billie leaned over to Sully. "Tara Trent was an animal rights activist," she said. "And she was a vegan, vehemently opposed to meat production."

"How do you know this?" Sully asked her as Frank's speech was coming to an end.

"First, because she told me as much at her interview that wasn't really an interview, and second because when I looked online to understand why someone might want to poison me with toxic mushrooms, I found a discussion board with her photo next to a profile," Billie explained. "It is still on my laptop in my office."

"I still don't understand," Sully said. "How do you know you were poisoned with toxic mushrooms?"

"I wanted to tell you before, but I had to tend to a cheese emergency for my business." She quietly explained what Doctor Hughes had told her.

"What exactly did this discussion board say?"

"Tara Trent, or who I think was Tara, led a discussion about using toxic mushrooms to make a group of people sick," Billie said. "She wrote about this less than one week ago, Sully. I think she showed up here to check things out for herself and when I confused her for Julie Neilson, she took advantage of the time and place to conduct a little rehearsal for what she planned to do here. Either that or she figured that poisoning the owner of the grounds might cause things to be put to a halt."

"What are we talking about here?" Asher asked.

"We're talking about a motive for why your girlfriend was poisoned by a perfect stranger," Sully said.

"And why was that?" Frank Price appeared behind Asher. "Why were you poisoned? Sorry but I couldn't help but overhear. I need to make sure my people aren't going to be killed by your staff."

"It seems an anti-meat activist decided to perform a dry run on what she planned to do here when I mistook her for someone else," Billie said. She eyed Frank carefully.

"I think you knew something was going to happen. Maybe not exactly what it was, but the way you acted when we first met and when you found out we'd hired a new chef had me feeling a little off about you. You've been in this industry a long time, and you said we couldn't trust anyone. That's why you kept coming around to make sure everything was okay. It was because you expected something bad to happen. This isn't your first rodeo, as they say."

Frank shook his head. "You see the turnout we

have here right after opening the gates," he said, sweeping his hands around. "Of course, I wanted to make sure things were going smoothly. What happened at my past events has nothing to do with what happened here."

"I can see that," Billie said. "And I can also see why it's enough to put a stop to the woman determined to put a stop to your event before she even has a chance to do any damage."

"What are you talking about, Billie?" Asher said. She could feel his grip tighten on her arm.

"I'm talking about the fact that Frank knew things were brewing here." She could see Frank's skin redden under his tall cowboy hat.

"Are you making an accusation here?" Sully asked, moving closer.

Billie turned to the detective. It was all starting to make sense. Tara hadn't threatened Julie at all. Julie just didn't want the job and her odd reaction was likely because Billie kept pressing her for information. She'd spent too much time overthinking and not enough time seeing what was right in front of her face.

"I don't know, but it makes sense, doesn't it? Frank kept acting squirrely every single time he was around us. It was as though he knew someone would come out here to cause trouble. Someone like Tara Trent."

"Dagummit," Frank muttered under his breath. "I knew you fools were affiliated with her in some way."

"How did you know that, Mr. Price?" Sully asked. "And what does it matter?"

"I have my sources," Frank said. "And that's all you need to know."

"You knew Tara Trent was in town," Billie continued. "And you knew that she had something big planned. She made that plain on the internet if you knew where to look and I bet you do. Is that right?"

"No comment." Frank shook his head.

Billie wanted to keep pushing until he broke. "I gave her the perfect opportunity to test out what she had planned when I confused her for the food truck manager who decided not to take the job. That's when she tested her theory that a little toxic mushroom goes a long way in a burger. If she could find a way in here, she could make a massive amount of folks sick at your event."

"And she would have done it, too," Frank hissed. "Nobody can blame me for trying to stop her."

Billie let out a sigh of relief.

"Only you didn't just stop her, Mr. Price," Sheriff

Avery said. "You murdered her. And now you are under arrest for killing Tara Trent."

Frank hung his head. When he looked up, he moved his hat to one side with his finger and grinned at the sheriff. "You sound like a local boy yourself," he said. "Surely we can do this somewhere else. Like inside that big building right there? I don't want to ruin this for the rest of the ranchers."

Billie stepped back out of the way to make room for the sheriff and Chief Abernathy to escort him away. Frank turned back to Billie as they walked away. "Hey, Halifax, you're lucky I'm not getting away with this. I don't take kindly to folks who outsmart me."

Billie leaned into Asher and watched as they walked the man away.

"I, for one, am very happy you outsmarted him," Asher said. "I really thought he was going to keep denying it. Honestly, I never would have guessed it was him."

"I didn't have to guess." Billie shrugged. "That man acted strangely from the get-go."

Asher chuckled. "If that's what you want to call it. Either way, great job."

"I'm not so sure I want to take credit here. I really messed up when I let Tara do what she did."

"That might be true, but it could have been much worse around here if she ended up with access to everyone. I hate to say that I'm glad she made you sick but…"

Billie laughed. "Really?"

"I mean, it was for the greater good. You took one for the team."

She shook her head. "Hey, Asher. How do you feel about mushrooms?"

***

If you enjoyed Grilled to Bits and are looking for more food truck adventures, preorder Behind Your Bake, today!

AUTHOR'S NOTE

I'd love to hear your thoughts on my books, the storylines, and anything else that you'd like to comment on—reader feedback is very important to me. My contact information, along with some other helpful links, is listed on the next page. If you'd like to be on my list of "folks to contact" with updates, release and sales notifications, etc.… just shoot me an email and let me know. Thanks for reading!

Also…

… if you're looking for more great reads, Summer Prescott Books publishes several popular series by outstanding Cozy Mystery authors.

CONTACT GRETCHEN ALLEN

Visit my website for more information about new releases, upcoming projects, and be sure to check out my special Members Only section for extra freebies and fun!

Website: www.gretchenallen.com

Email: contact@gretchenallen.com

Visit the Summer Prescott Books website to find even more great reads!

16691548R00069